Postcards from Space

Terrie Leigh Relf

Alban Lake Publishing

Also by Terrie Leigh Relf

Novels:

Blood Journey*
The Sisterhood of the Blood Moon
The Waters of Nyr

Poetry Collections:

My Friend, the Poet
An Untoward Bliss of Moons

* With Henry Lewis Sanders

Author's Note and Acknowledgements

Much of the work in this collection has been previously published in a variety of speculative and science fiction zines such as *Illumen, Scifaikuest,and Star*Line*. A few may have been slightly edited from the original.

There are a variety of poetic forms here: haibun, scifaiku sequences, solo zip rengays, free-verse, and others.

Thank you for reading.

Sincerely,

Terrie Leigh Relf
October 2019

Dedicated to Tyree Campbell

Table of Contents

Final Delivery

TO: The Remaining Residents of Hauran Colony VII

FROM: Teru Flare, Assistant to the Boortean Ambassador

DATE: Hauran Year 2030

RE: Final Delivery of Postcards from Space

We found postcards with the remains... a few tucked inside the pockets of all-terrain suits; others, bound together with the hems of old T-shirts. Then there were several inside an old dry rations bag of oats.

As you know, there are no postal services in space. No envelopes or stamps. No mailboxes. It appears the interim post-master must have saved them for delivery for when she returned.

They're all amazingly well-preserved. Of course, we read them, just in case some someone relayed classified information or something else above your pay grades.

It is our sincerest hope that these post-cards bring you some idea of the marvelous adventures shared by our collective peoples. And yes, some comfort as well.

Terrie Leigh Relf

Meet Me at Our Special Place on Terzon IV

The wind is fierce
as he steps into the tailor's shop
wanders the aisles in search of her

among spools and bolts
of finest Mora silk
bins of buttons and clasps
carved from banned Torka shell.

There's a letter tucked inside
his flight jacket, its edges
worn and frayed...

> *Meet me at that shop on Terzon IV.*
> *Please—just this one more time...*

A scent drifts toward him
from the fitting rooms...
sugared Mora blossoms
honey-glazed Tula nuts
an exotic spice from Taari.

Could it be... her?

He follows the scents
like fingers beckoning,
letter still in hand as
the tailor emerges with a customer,
an aging woman unknown to him.

He smiles at her politely, nods,
as is customary on this world,
the hope that was briefly kindled, now
dashed...

this could *not* be his longed-for love.

"A woman came, left this," the tailor says,
hands him an envelope of precious paper,
his name wrought in priceless ink.

He reaches out to grasp it,
offers murmured thanks,
buys a spool of crimson thread...

The customer averts her eyes as
with trembling hands
he opens the envelope,
reads a verse, at first confusing...

> *preserved in ice*
> *the scent of Mora blossoms*

but then its meaning dawns.

He smiles through wisdom's unshed tears,
and without a backward glance,
passes through the tailor's door
into a wind less fierce
than the memory of *her* scent.

Terrie Leigh Relf

The Crystal Caves of Io

We're planning to go sightseeing today. Wish you were here. Despite the frigid temperatures, our guide said he wanted to take us to a rather unique series of crystal caves.

>thermal suits
>the echo
>of ragged breathing

Once we stepped through the opening, I started to ask if the caves were safe, but our guide shushed me with a gloved appendage.

>orbs hovering
>lightning streaks
>of white light

Before our guide leads us into the main cavern, he rechecks our safety harnesses, clips us together, then to him.

>embedded in crystal
>an aurora borealis
>dark passages

We descend further into the latticework of caves. I capture a few images, hope they'll turn out.

rest stop
my gloved hand
alights on a skull

Terrie Leigh Relf

Within a Storm, Waiting

It is almost time to land...
but there are humans, pointing
toward the cacophonous eye of the storm;
zigzags of lightning broil brilliant green and
fuchsia,
molten, with shocks of gold.

It is near time to land,
but there are humans, watching
this cloud bank glows crimson in response;
oh how they gather,
clamoring for images, vidfeed,
curious, as to whom we are.

It is time we landed,
but there are humans, gathering,
so we search for an alternate route;
with ciphony, our vocal communiqués
disguised... silent, even as we ascend.

It is past time to land.
Within this uncertain storm, waiting,
I write this postcard to you
remaining hopeful you'll understand...
what I needed to say was left unsaid.

Stasis Dreaming

At first, it is dark in the stasis chamber. So dark that you wander through memories like black-and-white photos, but only the black appears, with negative, but no positive space.

  ganglia reach out
  their tendrilled arms
  sensation

After a few hours, or perhaps it is only moments, as time moves differently in stasis, the brain and mind adjust. Vivid colors begin to seep within your dreams.

  turquoise moons
  the way starlight
  turns our flesh golden

Then, sound... The murmur of voices guiding you toward a doorway. Just a few more steps... a few more steps...

  neural symphony
  how the cadenza
  goes on and on

Terrie Leigh Relf

On Learning New Customs

The Boortean Survey Station is on autopilot.
Samples have been gathered, catalogued,
discussed. The cultural ambassador is on
Haura, learning about their customs.

    alien concepts
    a hand-delivered postcard
    from Haura

The ambassador has brought Hauran gifts!
She pours colored pencils and pens, paper,
around the cartographer's station. We
scribble for a while, attempt self-portraits.

    the scent of Mora blossoms
    wafts through the air vents
    homesick

Mindgrid communiqué arrives. The mission
has been extended through summer. Morale
fluctuates.

    so many flavors
    of Hauran ice cream
    synthsuit too tight

News Alert! December 21, 2012 is less than one year and three months away...

Some say the Mayans were seers who foretold the end of the world, but they left earth early just in case they made an error in calculation.

> how the mind
> glitters more than gold
> Spanish invaders

Others claim, "The Apocalypse is NOW," and are already building bunkers, stockpiling food and water, gathering arms and munitions.

> solar flares
> how global satellites
> turn to ash

There's this guy who lives on the corner who still has a ticket to ride from the OB Spaceman. He wants to hold a séance to see if it's okay to bring his girlfriend.

> green flash at sunset
> scent of patchouli
> tinfoil helmets

Another neighbor is a stockbroker trading futures for today.

contemplating scurvy
in zero-g
hydroponic tomatoes

The Neighborhood Watch Program is hosting a disaster preparedness seminar. The children are kept busy making starships and aliens out of orange-scented fluorescent clay.

survival gear camouflaged
the scent of chocolate
chip cookies

My family's already in the desert, but I haven't heard from them for a while. It's possible they aren't receiving signals. When you arrive, be sure to remind them to turn left, then proceed to the landing zone. If you miss the transport, there's a portal buried beneath that meteor. Don't worry about the odd hum or high-voltage arcs, as they're really just for show.

please don't feed
the humans...
postcards from space

On Survey Station B379: Rotation V

just past dawn   an empty spaceport
  the whirr   of stasis chambers

she dreams   of abandonment   scent of
jasmine

miners   too long in the dark
weighing in   always weighing in

remembering   beer   when
spring followed winter

his breath   against the nape of her
neck
all those letters   unread

alternating temperatures   cold
      colder

moving toward us a cluster of stars
come nightfall   three new moons

How to Deal with Boredom while Working Aboard Hauran Survey Station B23791

The Boortean Ambassador's assistant was reading the most recent edition of *Time Travel for Dummies* in an attempt to ignore the precarious pile of satellite feed that needed to be transferred into the data base.

> those Haurans
> and their multi-tasking
> snack time

The compactor whirred into action, whined, then emitted a noxious odor before pulverizing its contents into a vaporous ash.

> all tangled up
> with strings
> shooting star

Wondering where to go on leave, the Ambassador's assistant pulled out a Hauran child's globe, spun it around and around and around until it broke free and attempted to find a stable orbit.

> logging in
> to her SpaceFace page
> spamspamspam

Winter Celebrations
on Lunar Colony 8

the scent of pine
from the hydroponic gardens
solstice tree saplings

habitat skylight
a garland of stars
draped just so

scraping frost
from the generators
remembering the taste of snow...

boxes of old
summer clothes
quilting bee

knowing the difference
between wants and needs
a box of tea from Earth

letters bound
with red ribbon
smudged ink

The Trip Home

The Alpha Centaurian said, "we've finally come to take you home. You're allowed one carry-on bag." And so the exiled female went from cupboard to drawer, scanned, then emptied the contents of a shelf into a galactic-issue carry-all bag. There wasn't much she really wanted to bring with her, but she took what she thought she'd need.

    sucked dry of oxygen
    folded into triangles
    earth

The Truth About Oregon

Some say that people who visit Oregon are never heard of again. They go for a visit, seem to like it there, so stay.

> vacationing
> in rural America
> not even a postcard

But I just learned it's the fog that gets them, the fog and that incessant rain... They wander about, get lost, and nature's tears wash all remnants of their existence away.

> just beyond the trees
> beacon lights
> scent of pine

Other people say, "That's ludicrous! It's not the fog or the rain, but a multi-dimensional portal that disappears them." "It's part of a government conspiracy, too," some whisper beneath their breath.

> making deals
> with alien visitors
> redwoods on the moon

Come to think of it, why believe anything anyone says about Oregon—especially those Oregonians who managed to escape to warmer, less humid climes.

a thousand hours
of morning cartoons
satellite malfunction

Still, aren't you curious? I know I am...

one-way ticket
to Portland
no refunds

Interim Field Report

Artifact No. 29014: After the polar caps melted, and slush gave way to rock, rock to caves thought hidden for one-thousand years or more, the excavation team discovered what at first appeared to be a clay tablet.

>parabolic functions—
>alien treatise
>emitting light

Artifact No. 73159: After the partial thaw, once the core samples were tested and retested, and a volunteer was found from among the new settlers' most promising candidates, the scientific community was appropriately cautious before declaring what they believed may eventually prove to be an evolutionary triumph.

>searching ancient archives
>for correlative data:
>what is a baby?

Artifact No. 99371-b: After the waters receded, and temporary shelters were replaced with more permanent habitats, the scientific community spread out to repopulate the planet.

>clinging to the
>cavern walls
>unknown genus

Terrie Leigh Relf

It Wasn't Silly Putty

Late last night, a cargo box was abandoned on the off-ramp to a local park. A packing statement found at the scene was labeled as children's toys, but none of the merchandise was located. Torn packaging of indeterminate origin was also located in trash bins at the nearby park, along with a pink gooey residue. Since no one has come forward to claim ownership, investigators are perplexed as to what occurred and who might be to blame.

> taking imprints
> of our children
> alien archeologist

Excerpts from a Series of Trans-Galactic Communiqués

Milky Way
kindergarten students
composing messages

swimming beneath the stars... a school of
Koi

summer storm
revising transmissions
for Gliese 667

lightyears come and go... retirement
postponed

exoplanets
how atmospheric conditions
inspire hope

streaming science fiction reruns... METI
campaign

Swirl

She was in the process of summer cleaning—
going through closets and cupboards,
rearranging what was left over while stacking
up bins to shuttle over to the Veterans of
Alien Wars office, when lightning struck.

> mismatched socks
> an old boot
> memories of Earth

At first, the sky outside the storm windows
of her domed habitat reminded her of
Chinese mustard, the kind she used to buy
in a tin on Earth. A light dusting of powder
that swirled on the breeze, a light dusting of
powder that soon became pasty as it
descended through the mist.

> no place for love
> but still his voice
> lingers

After a while, it seemed that the sky had
rearranged itself, become something else,
something other than sky. She remembered
reading a book once, *The Red Badge of
Courage*... red... blood red like oranges and
the multihued sands that swirled just
beyond the protective field.

sleepless nights—
if only the sirens
knew her name

22

Phosphorus

It takes imagination to create a world where the scent of phosphorus is enticing. At first, the scent is revolting until someone turns a kaleidoscope just so...

Be careful not to appropriate—or misappropriate—another planet's cultural oddities, especially when it's ludicrous to assume we can be truly objective. Oh we can try, but seriously, we're just fooling ourselves.

does
the
singularity
dream
us
or
do
we
dream
the
singularity?

Archaeological Survey: Site Undisclosed

The dig team assembled and set to work. Shovels and trowels, screens and brushes, their bodies bent beneath the heat of morning sun.

> surprisingly intact
> it resembles
> an ancient monastery

Stepping through an arched entryway, helmet beams on low, the team assembles in the anteroom, proceeds toward a central hall. Too many corridors; not a single door.

> subsonic vibration
> sensors recalibrated
> tech crew on alert

The air is unexpectedly free of dust. No evidence of previous inhabitants or burial chambers. Bare walls and barren shelves. Not a single artifact.

> crumbling earth
> the rise of
> fresher air

Reconvening in the central hall, the team leader divides his crew into teams to explore a specified quadrant. They return to digging.

final report
the scent of
redacted ink

Attempting to pass the time...

Nearly home, we clean the starship from stem to stern, conduct a supply inventory, complete the required reports.

> data update
> the Tyraelian recipe
> for beer

With time to spare, we reminisce about our travels, and those among us who still pray, call upon their deities for a safe landing. Others just hope that there is someone there to greet us at the station.

> repacking our trunks
> finding space
> for souvenirs and gifts

While our ship remains in geosynchronous orbit, we release several survey vessels. They are unable to confirm landing coordinates or establish communication with ground control.

> drones conduct a flyby
> where land once was
> only water remains

Terrie Leigh Relf

Homecoming

After all those years in orbit, we're nearly
home. The world we left, a curiosity looming.
Just outside the port screen, our previous
world so close we can almost touch its
altered landscape.

> far out to sea
> a docking bay
> wet landing

They didn't expect us to return, either then
or now, and yet here we are. Formalities
aside, we receive a private debriefing, a full
work-up, and a series of vaccinations before
taking leave.

> joking aside
> gravity really
> is a bitch

In our absence, much had changed. As we
ventured to the stars, our trans-galactic
allies decided to revisit Earth and live among
us now that we'd supposedly evolved.

> rising above the sea
> curious architecture
> vertigoic landscape

Next time, perhaps we should use their portal. Then again, there's just something about traveling amongst the stars.

>reading postcards
>from space
>still longing to return

Blood Journey
Henry Lewis Sanders and Terrie Leigh Relf

Blood Journey is an intricately constructed tale of love and revenge among the undead. The behading of the evil Baroness Andora by Count Vasilie sets off a chain of events among the followers of the Church of the Dark Mother that threatens to destroy the vampire community. Relf and Sanders follow the trail of blood and darkness that began long ago and far away as they weave an erotic path through the exotic nights of London, lust, ad mayhem to slake the thirst of eve the most avid readers of the Dark Side.

Only $9.95
Available from www.irbstore.co

Sisterhood of the Blood Moon
by Terrie Leigh Relf

For thousands of Earth years, the Transgalactic Consortium has had a quiet interest in this planet and its inhabitants, the Haurans. While the Sisterhood of the Blood Moon works together with the Consortium and Haurans to maintain balance in the universe, the Blood Moon is fast approaching. The power of this moon reveals untold secrets... including a sacred covenant with the Mora Spiders. There is an ancient pact that needs to be honored—but at what cost and for whose purpose? The world may come to an end. But will there be a chance for a new beginning?

Only $14.95
Available from www.irbstore.co

Waters of Nyr
by Terrie Leigh Relf

Cassandra and Baron are just ordinary teen-agers when they meet in a community college art class and discover that they have a lot in common.

It doesn't take long for Cassandra and Baron to discover that there are no coincidences—and they are far from ordinary. They barely escape being abducted by shapeshifters, their grand-mothers go missing, and a mysterious group of men appear to whisk them away to safety—aboard a starslip to another galaxy.

Only $10.95
Available from www.irbstore.co

An Untoward Bliss of Moons
by Terrie Leigh Relf

It's her poetic tour de force. Nobody ever wrote poetry like this. Nobody else writes it now. Ms. Relf not only takes the view from beyond the left field fence, she does it from a stadium in another galaxy. From "A Poet on Board" to "Why there are no poets on board" and "And so we set sail to Alpha Centauri," Ms Relf is at once poignant, amusing, acerbic, witty, charming, gauche, and sexy. In the universe of science fiction and fantasy poetry, she is nonpareil.

Only $5.95
Available from www.irbstore.co

Order Your Books Today!

Book	Price	Amount	Total
Blood Journey	$9.95		
Sisterhood of the Blood Moon	$14.95		
Waters of Nyr	$10.95		
An Untoward Bliss of Moons	$5.95		
		Subtotal	$
		Shipping	$9.70
		Final Total	$

Name: ____
Address: ____
City: ____
State: ____
Zip: ____
Phone: ____
Date: ____

Checks or money orders need to be made out to Alban Lake Publishing.

For Credit Card Orders:
Card #: ____
Exp. Date: ____
Security Code: _______________________________________
Date: ____
Signature: ____

Alban Lake Publishing
P.O. Box 141
Colo, IA 50056-014
515-357-8910 (texts welcome)
albanlake@yahoo.com
Website: www.albanlakepublishing.com